Beast Quest®

MASTER YOUR DESTINY

THE DAGGER OF DOOM

With special thanks to Elizabeth Galloway

For the Broadway Crew: Amanda, Catherine, Emma, Jo, Karen, Kate and Sam

www.beastquest.co.uk

ORCHARD BOOKS
338 Euston Road, London NW1 3BH
Orchard Books Australia
Level 17/207 Kent St, Sydney, NSW 2000

A Paperback Original
First published in Great Britain in 2011

Beast Quest is a registered trademark of Beast Quest Limited
Series created by Working Partners Limited, London

Text © Beast Quest Limited 2011
Cover and inside illustrations by Steve Sims © Orchard Books 2011

A CIP catalogue record for this book is available from
the British Library.

ISBN 978 1 40831 406 7

7 9 10 8

Printed and bound by CPI Group (UK) Ltd, Croydon, CR0 4YY

The paper and board used in this paperback are natural recyclable
products made from wood grown in sustainable forests. The
manufacturing processes conform to the environmental regulations
of the country of origin.

Orchard Books is a division of Hachette Children's Books,
an Hachette UK company.

www.hachette.co.uk

MASTER YOUR DESTINY

THE DAGGER OF
DooM

BY ADAM BLADE

ORCHARD

Gorgonia is doomed! Our realm has long been plagued by Malvel, the Dark Wizard.

A brave band of rebels swore to free the land from his evil. They forged the Dagger of Doom from a shard of argentium, a magical metal with protective powers.

But now the Dark Wizard has stolen the Dagger, and created two terrifying Beasts — Marlik the Drowning Terror and Klaxa the Armoured Enemy — to attack the rebels. Gorgonia is at Malvel's mercy...

But word of our troubles has reached Avantia. Tom has sworn to help us, and he has a new companion on his Beast Quest — YOU. Can you defeat the Beasts and reclaim the Dagger — before it's too late?

Kerlo, Gatekeeper of Gorgonia

1

Bright sunlight dances on the surface of the Western Ocean. You, Tom and Elenna are in a fishing boat. Elenna swings the large sail round, catching the breeze.

"Here's perfect," she says.

You heave the fishing net up from the deck. But before you can drop it into the water, a dark shape appears on the horizon.

"It's a rowing boat," you say.

Elenna steers alongside it. A girl lies slumped at the bottom, her red hair covering her face.

You and Tom reach down and lift her into your own boat.

"She's from Gorgonia," says Tom, pointing to the silver talisman around her neck. "All the Gorgonian rebels wear one of these."

Elenna picks up a flask of water. She kneels next to the girl, smoothing her hair from her face.

Both Tom and Elenna gasp.

"Odora!" cries Tom. "We met her many Quests ago."

Odora's eyelids flutter. "The evil one...he's stolen it..." Then she passes out again.

You sail back to shore and carry Odora onto the beach. Silver, Elenna's pet wolf, is crouched beside your weapons. Tom's horse, Storm, and your horse, Lightning, whinny uneasily.

The air shimmers and a gigantic gateway appears, formed from the jaws of Trillion the Three-Headed Lion.

"The way into Gorgonia," says Tom.

"I think Odora was trying to tell us that something's happened there," you say. "Come on – let's find out what!"

You and Tom grab your swords and shields, and place Odora across Storm's back. You lead the way through the gate. A blinding light flashes and a bolt of energy shoots through you.

When your vision clears, Avantia has gone. Instead, you stand in Gorgonia, on a rocky slope under a red sky.

A figure sits hunched on a rock, his back to you. Across his knees rests a long cane, the strap of an eye-patch stretched across his bald scalp. His cloak flaps in the wind.

"Kerlo the Gatekeeper," mutters Tom. "He guards the way into the Dark Realm."

Should you approach Kerlo – or sneak past him into Gorgonia?

⚔ *Choose your destiny* ⚔

To approach Kerlo, turn to **29**.

To enter Gorgonia without approaching Kerlo,

turn to **40**.

2

You and Tom lead the rebels into the sweltering rainforest. The damp air makes it difficult to breathe.

You swat at the insects that buzz around you. One nips your shoulder, but as you turn to swat it away, you see it's a bat!

With a terrible screech, a swarm of bats descends through the trees. They snatch at the rebels with their claws.

"Hurry!" you yell, urging Lightning into a canter.

You beat the bats away with your shield as you charge out of the rainforest – emerging in front of the Western City. The huge black gates that lead inside are closed.

"How do we get in?" Tom wonders.

Glancing around, you see a fallen tree you could use as a battering ram, and a gigantic catapult streaked with slime.

⊰⊱ *Choose your destiny* ⊰⊱
*To use the battering ram, turn to **19**.*
*To use the catapult, turn to **26**.*

3

"Come on, Kaymon," you yell, drawing your sword. "You don't frighten us!"

The Beast crouches low to the ground. With a snarl she springs at you, saliva dripping from her fangs. Tom raises his shield but Kaymon's weight sends him sprawling onto the flagstones. You lash out with your blade, slicing a nick in her side.

Kaymon howls with rage. Her massive shoulders ripple and contort, then the Beast's body splits apart. You gasp with horror. Now there isn't just one Kaymon – there are three!

One of the hounds strikes your sword aside with her enormous paw. Her fangs snare your jerkin, but you yank the fabric away. From the corner of your eye you see the other two hounds chase Tom up onto the jagged battlements. *How can we possibly defeat three Beasts?*

The Beast backs you up against one of the pillars that surround the courtyard. You grab a rock and smash it over her

head. You leap aside and she staggers into
the pillar. It crashes on top of her and she
thrashes beneath it, growling.

In the centre of the courtyard is a
metal ring, embedded into the ground.
A trapdoor! Could it be a way out of
the castle?

You glance up to where Tom is struggling against the other two Kaymons. If you both die, the Quest will be over. But can you leave your friend behind?

Choose your destiny

To leave Tom and go through the trapdoor,
turn to **51**.
To stay and help Tom, turn to **54**.

4

You and Tom leave the horses by the shore and climb up the bone ladder. It arches over the foul moat, to a window halfway up the tallest turret of the ruined castle. The rungs feel greasy under your fingers.

Snap! Your foot goes straight through one of the rungs.

"Hurry," urges Tom beneath you.

You scramble up and a gnarled hand reaches through the window. You have no choice but to take it.

It belongs to an old woman in a black cape. She pulls first you and then Tom into a dark stone room. Then she takes a glassy orb from her cloak.

"A seeing stone," whispers Tom. "She's a soothsayer – one who tells the future."

The woman hisses, "Follow me." She walks out of the room to a stone staircase.

⟞⟝ *Choose your destiny* ⟞⟝
To follow the soothsayer, turn to **9.**

To refuse to follow the soothsayer, turn to **16**.

5

You sound a ringing blast on the horn, and the rebels turn towards you. A man holding an axe yells, "Watch out!"

You spin round to see Marlik leap from the bushes. One of his arms turns into a jet of water, which he shoots at your face. You choke, blinded for a moment. Tom jumps in front of you, using his shield to deflect the water, then swings it at the Beast's head. Marlik topples to the ground, his tentacles writhing.

The rebel with the axe rushes over. "We'll finish him off," he says. "You'd better go after Malvel. He's taken the Dagger to the Western City."

You thank the rebels and canter away. On the outskirts of the City are burning buildings and injured people.

"Malvel's path of destruction," you mutter grimly.

The road you're moving along slopes underground, becoming a network of tunnels. The horses' hooves ring on the stone floor and the torches on the walls cast eerie shadows.

Mocking laughter echoes around you.

"I'd know that sound anywhere," says Tom. "It's Malvel!"

Should you hide – or follow the Dark Wizard?

Choose your destiny

To hide from Malvel, turn to **38**.

To follow Malvel, turn to **42**.

"We're not giving you our horses," you tell the boy. "Besides, shouldn't you help us for the good of Gorgonia?"

The boy's face twists with fury and his fists clench.

You quickly think of a plan. "Alright," you pretend to agree. "But we'll only give you the horses if you take us to the ruined castle."

To your relief, the boy nods. "It's a deal."

He walks over the rocky terrain, you and Tom riding behind.

"I'm not handing over Storm," Tom whispers, his forehead furrowed in confusion.

"Don't worry," you reply. "We're not really giving him our horses! We'll canter ahead as soon as we see the castle."

The boy suddenly disappears into a hole in the rocky ground. "Help!" he shouts.

You leap from Lightning's back and peer inside. The boy is thrashing about, his limbs contorted.

"We've got to get him out of there,"
says Tom, springing down beside you.

But as you watch the boy flail,
uneasiness pools in your stomach.

Choose your destiny

To help the boy out of the hole, turn to **18**.

To leave the boy in the hole, turn to **32**.

7

You and Tom step inside the room filled with armour.

"Where did all this come from?" you wonder.

"Malvel stole it," says a familiar voice.

You spin round. "Elenna!" you cry.

"How did you get here?" Tom asks.

Elenna grins. "Aduro sent me. He knew you two could do with my help. Come on," she says. "I saw Malvel while I was searching for you. He had the Dagger tucked into his belt. He was heading above ground."

You all dash out of the room – but freeze when you hear a clanking sound.

"Is that a Beast?" you ask. "We should find out."

But Elenna shakes her head. "The Dagger's more important."

Choose your destiny

To do as Elenna says, turn to 12.

To investigate the noise, turn to 27.

8

You roll through the clinging mud, grabbing your sword. Klaxa bellows as she thunders past, just missing you. You leap up and stand by Tom. Your eyes scan the Beast's body, searching for a weakness. Her flanks are covered in plates of hide, like a suit of armour.

"Aim for her eyes and her belly," you tell Tom.

As Klaxa charges again, you both thrust your swords at her. She tosses her head and your blade bounces off her horn. Purple liquid drips down the metal.

Storm and Lightning back into the prickly copse, snorting with terror. The thorny branches reach down towards them like bony hands, snaring the end of Lightning's tail. Your horse thrashes in panic, but her tail only becomes more entangled. Klaxa's eyes fix on Lightning, drool pouring from her jaws.

As the Beast charges your horse, you hurl your sword. The blade slices through

the end of Lightning's tail, and she canters
free. Klaxa gives a surprised grunt as she
crashes into the copse. The prickly
branches coil round her, holding her tight.

"Let's go!" shouts Tom.

You gallop towards the ruined castle on
the horizon. "That's just the kind of place
where Malvel would hide the Dagger,"
you say.

The castle is surrounded by a wide moat. A tall ladder stretches from the bank, one end resting against the castle wall. Its rungs are made from bone. A small boat bobs in the stagnant water.

How should you reach the castle?

Choose your destiny

To climb the ladder, turn to **4.**

To use the boat, turn to **36.**

9

You and Tom follow the soothsayer up the spiral stone staircase to the top of the turret, and into a chamber.

It's been ransacked. The wooden chests are open with nothing inside. An empty glass case hangs on the wall.

"This was the Gorgonian treasure room," says the soothsayer. "The rebels used it to fund their war against Malvel. But he stole everything." She points to the glass case. "That held the Dagger of Doom."

The soothsayer holds up the seeing stone. The orb is misty, and you and Tom gasp in wonder as an image appears inside. It shows rows of tents, with men and women laughing and talking. Then the image fades and is replaced by another – the face of Malvel.

"What does it mean?" you ask.

"The Dark Wizard is at the rebel camp of Kaloom," she explains. "He has the Dagger."

The soothsayer leads you and Tom back

down the staircase. It winds deep underground, then becomes a tunnel.

"This is the way back to your horses," she says. "Good luck, young warriors. Gorgonia depends on you."

When you reach the rebel camp, you shelter behind some bushes so you can watch what's happening. The rebels moving around the tents each wear a silver talisman about their necks, just like Odora's.

A tall man in a long cloak and hood walks towards the camp.

"Let's tell him we're here to help," says Tom.

But you can't see a talisman around the man's neck. Can you trust him?

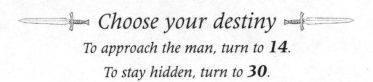

Choose your destiny

*To approach the man, turn to **14**.*

*To stay hidden, turn to **30**.*

10

"The whole of Avantia is proud of you," says King Hugo, smiling.

You, Tom, Elenna and Aduro are enjoying a feast with the King. The table is laden with roast potatoes, cuts of meat and an enormous cake. Storm and Lightning are in the stables outside, having a well-earned meal of oats.

Elenna tosses a chicken leg to Silver, who lies at her feet. She sighs. "I can't believe I missed such an exciting Quest."

Aduro chuckles as he hands everyone a slice of cake. "I'm sure there'll be plenty more Quests to come."

Tom nods. Through a mouthful of food, he says, "Malvel may be gone for now, but he'll be back."

"And we'll be waiting for him," you say.

The End

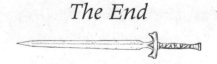

11

You kick the table and the flagon falls to the ground, shattering.

You use the shards to slice through the ropes that bind your wrists and ankles, then free Tom. Lifting the fabric wall of the tent, you crawl out. You're relieved to find your confiscated swords stuck into the grass, your shields beside them.

You duck behind a crowd of rebels as Malvel approaches the tent. He peers inside the entrance flap and his face darkens.

"They've escaped!" he snarls. Tucked into his belt is a blade with a skull set into the hilt. The Dagger of Doom!

The rebels cry out with fear as a shadow falls over the camp. It's a monstrous flying horse, swooping down on gigantic wings, its teeth snapping ferociously.

"Skor," mutters Tom.

The Beast lands and Malvel leaps onto its back. "To the Western City!" he demands.

"We've got to follow him," you say. "And

we should take the rebels with us."

Tom nods. But which is the safest route to the city?

===➤ *Choose your destiny* ➤===

To travel through the humid rainforest,

*turn to **2**.*

To travel through the shadowy forest,

*turn to **23**.*

12

You and Tom follow Elenna into a side chamber. Leaning against the far wall is a ladder; you climb up and through a hatch, into a banqueting hall. An enormous wooden table stretches the length of the room, and at the far end is a cauldron bubbling over a fire.

On the table is a silver platter filled with water. Blue gas swirls above it.

"This looks like Aduro's magic," says Elenna. "Maybe he's got a message for us."

You hurry towards it. The surface shimmers, but Aduro doesn't appear. Instead, the water shoots up into a rippling column. It solidifies into a Beast with a muscular torso, and arms and legs covered with green scales. A hideous wreath of tentacles sprouts through its neck, and it opens its mouth in a terrible roar, revealing rows of teeth like deadly knives.

"Glad you could join us, Marlik the Drowning Terror!" laughs Malvel. He has been hiding behind the table!

The Beast leaps from the table onto Tom, pinning his arms to his sides.

Elenna shoots an arrow at Marlik, slicing through one of his tentacles. The Beast snarls at her and you charge, as Tom gets to his feet. Your sword slashes Marlik's scaly skin and he leaps onto the table, near the spitting cauldron. You have an idea...

"Get him in the cauldron!" you yell.

Tom picks up a jug and hurls it at the Beast, but it only grazes his shoulder.

You grab the silver platter. Your muscles tensed, you send it spinning through the air. It hits Marlik in the chest. He wobbles on the edge of the table, then tips into the cauldron. He gives a roar of pain and his body melts into a green liquid.

"You did it!" Elenna cries.

"Well done," sneers the Dark Wizard. "But now comes the real test."

He pulls the Dagger of Doom from his belt and rams the tip into the wooden table. His eyes bore into your own. "Let's fight for the Dagger," he says. "One on one."

Choose your destiny

To refuse to fight Malvel, turn to **31**.

To fight Malvel, turn to **39**.

13

Leaving the rebel camp behind, you and Tom retrieve Storm and Lightning and gallop after Malvel, towards the Western City. But you're barely out of sight of the tents when you hear a ferocious roar.

"The rebels are being attacked!" you call across to Tom.

You rush back to the camp. In the middle of the tents is a gigantic Beast. She stands on four legs as sturdy as tree trunks. Shades of grey and silver swirl over the Beast's armoured flanks. A horn juts from her forehead.

Malvel's mocking voice seems to hang on the air. *Fear Klaxa the Armoured Enemy...*

Klaxa tramples through the camp, goring the tents with her horn. She stabs it into a rebel's chest; foam froths from his mouth and he sinks to the ground. Purple liquid spouts from the horn's tip.

"Poison," you gasp.

You leap from your horse and charge at Klaxa, but she bats you aside with her massive head, knocking your sword from your hand. A rebel warrior with an axe tosses it back.

"Can I borrow that?" you ask.

He passes you the weapon. As Klaxa thunders towards you, you swing the axe at her horn. But she swerves aside and it slashes her shoulder instead. The Beast bellows in pain and rears up. When her front legs crash to the ground you spring onto her flank, still gripping the axe. You use the gaps between her armoured plates to climb up onto her back.

"Hold on!" shouts Tom.

Klaxa roars, tossing her head and shaking her body to try to throw you off. Gripping onto her back with your knees, you aim at her horn with the axe.

Thwack!

You slice it through. With a spurt of purple poison, the horn falls to the ground.

Klaxa sinks to her knees. You jump clear as her body collapses. The Beast melts into a bubbling, foaming mass and seeps into the ground. All that remains is a patch of scorched earth.

But there's no time to celebrate: you and Tom leave for the Western City. When you get there, the gates are locked. How will you get inside – by using a tree trunk as a battering ram, or the giant catapult that sits by the walls?

Choose your destiny

To use a battering ram, turn to **19**.
To use the catapult, turn to **26**.

14

The man strides towards the rebel tents, his face hidden in the shadow of his hood.

"Wait!" you call.

He stops, and you and Tom run towards him.

"We're here to help the Gorgonian rebels get the Dagger back," you explain.

Slowly, the man pulls down his hood, revealing a familiar, cruel face.

"Malvel!" you cry.

Both you and Tom draw your swords, but Malvel unsheathes a glittering blade with a skull set into the hilt.

"The Dagger of Doom!" you cry.

Malvel smirks. "Meddling fools," he sneers. "You were looking for the Dagger – and now you've found it!"

He lunges towards you, the blade's deadly tip aimed straight at your heart. You know that death awaits you...

Your Quest has failed. And Gorgonia will fall to Malvel...

15

You follow the trail of hoofprints through the swamp, the thick mud sucking at the horses' hooves. Yellow mist swirls around you, making your eyes sting.

The prints lead to a dark shadow on the horizon.

"It looks like woodland," you say.

Getting closer, you see the trees are covered in long spines. Beside them rests an enormous grey boulder.

Tom leaps from Storm's back, studying the ground. "The prints stop next to the boulder," he says.

You swing from Lightning's saddle and peer into the woodland. "I can't see the Beast anywhere. It's disappeared!"

Tom scrambles onto the boulder, his eyebrows knitted in thought. You climb up to sit next to him. "What should we do now?" you wonder.

Lightning gives a sudden snort and backs away from you, her nostrils flared. The boulder beneath you trembles and

shudders into life. It tosses you and Tom
into the air and you land beside the trees,
your sword flying from your hand. Fear
clenches your stomach as the rocky surface
shifts to become a terrible Beast. It stands
on four thick legs, its massive flanks
covered in bony plates. A horn juts from
its forehead, purple liquid dripping from
the tip. Its eyes glitter with rage.

Malvel's voice seems to whisper in your
ear: *Behold Klaxa the Armoured Enemy…*

"Malvel's Beast," says Tom grimly.

Klaxa gives a terrible roar, making the

prickly branches quiver. She lowers her
horn and thunders towards you. You must
think quickly. Do you grab the branch
above you, to pull yourself out of Klaxa's
range? Or should you lunge for your sword?

⚔ *Choose your destiny* ⚔

*To lunge for your sword, turn to **8**.*
*To grab the branch, turn to **48**.*

16

"No," you say to the soothsayer. "How do we know we can trust you?"

The soothsayer's face crumples with a wave of sadness. She drops the seeing stone, and it rolls across the flagstones.

"My foresight must be weakening," she sighs, sinking to the ground. "I thought you two would be the ones to save Gorgonia."

You kneel beside her and take her wrinkled hand. "We want to defeat Malvel. Please – tell us what we must do."

Her watery eyes shine with hope. She picks up the stone and shows you the image glowing inside it. You can make out rows of tents with ragged men and women milling around them.

"Gorgonian rebels," she says. "They will help you."

She points to a trapdoor in the courtyard floor. You climb down into a secret passageway that leads you out of the castle, back to Storm and Lightning, and ride to the rebel camp. Leaving the horses behind some bushes, you approach the tents.

Suddenly, strong hands seize your arms, clamping them to your sides. You feel a sharp pain in your skull, and everything goes dark…

When you open your eyes, you and Tom are lying inside a tent. Your hands are tied behind you and your ankles are bound.

"How are we going to get out of here?" Tom asks.

Your swords and shields are gone, so you look around for something to cut your bonds. There's a flagon of water you could smash to create sharp fragments. But do you have time? Should you crawl under the wall of the tent instead?

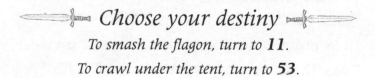

Choose your destiny

To smash the flagon, turn to **11**.
To crawl under the tent, turn to **53**.

17

You and Tom duck behind some bushes, Lightning and Storm with you, and spy on the rebels moving around the camp. Some crouch over fires, stirring cooking pots, while others sharpen swords or whittle arrows from branches. Their backs are bent and their eyelids droop.

"They look exhausted," Tom whispers.

"And lots of them are injured," you add, pointing to a man with a bandage around his arm. "Maybe they've already been fighting Malvel – or his Beasts."

A terrible scream tears through the camp.

"They're being attacked," you cry. You and Tom mount your horses and gallop through the tents. Your fist clenches angrily over the hilt of your sword when you see Marlik the Drowning Terror. The Beast hurls a rebel into one of the fires, then grabs hold of a girl about your own age. His arm changes into its watery form as he slides it down her throat. He's going to drown her...

"Let her go!" you yell. You snatch up a wooden tent pole and leap from the saddle onto Marlik's back, hooking it across his hideous, tentacled neck. The Beast gives a hiss of rage, gagging, and drops the girl. Tom grabs a cooking pot and clumps him on the head. Marlik falls to the ground, stunned.

"Thanks," says the girl, rubbing her neck.

"Is Malvel here, too?" you ask.

She shakes her head. "He's gone to the Western City – with the Dagger."

You turn to Tom. "Let's go."

You see a doorway cut into the jagged walls of the City. Leaving the horses out of sight behind a pile of rubble, you go through. You walk along an underground tunnel with two rooms at its end. One is filled with armour, the other treasure.

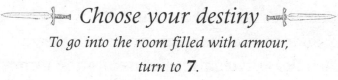

Choose your destiny

To go into the room filled with armour,
turn to 7.

To go into the room filled with treasure,
turn to 33.

18

You reach into the hole, stretching towards the boy. "Here. I'll pull you out."

The boy seizes your hand – but drags you into the hole beside him.

"Let go!" shouts Tom, staring over the edge.

But the boy's grip tightens. His skin turns green and scaly, and tentacles sprout from his neck. Tom tries to swipe him with his sword, but he knocks it away.

He's changing into a Beast! you realise.

The boy's body expands, bursting through his clothes. His mouth fills with rows of fangs.

You hear Malvel's mocking voice on the air. *Marlik the Drowning Terror is here…*

The Beast snarls and his body changes again. His legs become water, filling the hole. He's going to drown you!

Suddenly, a cane strikes Marlik's head. He releases you and slumps into the water.

"Kerlo!" you gasp.

The Gatekeeper grabs you and hauls you

out of the hole. His single eye flashes.

"Did you think I wouldn't notice you enter Gorgonia?" he says crossly. "Well – since you're the best hope we've got, you'd better take this."

He thrusts a horn into your hands.

"It's the Horn of Kaloom," Kerlo explains. "Use it to call for help next time." He jabs at the horizon with his cane. "The Dagger's that way."

Marlik stirs, his tentacles writhing.

"Go!" Kerlo orders. "Before the Beast awakes..."

You gallop across the plain to a ruined castle. "Maybe the Dagger's in there," you say.

The castle is circled by a moat. A rickety drawbridge hangs across it, and a series of rocks stick out of the water. Which way should you cross?

=══╬══ *Choose your destiny* ══╬══

To go over the drawbridge, turn to **45**.

To go over the rocks, turn to **52**.

"Push!" you yell. You, Tom and a group of rebels shove against a tree trunk. With a crack, the wood splinters and the tree falls.

Grabbing the end of the trunk, you direct them to slam it into the city gates.

Bang! The impact makes the tree shudder under your fingers. *Bang! Bang!*

The gates groan, springing open. You seize your horses and canter into the city.

You're shocked by the destruction around you. The buildings are blackened by flame. The only complete building is a

tower with jagged battlements around the top. Malvel's face appears at the uppermost window, creased into a wicked grin.

Skor the Winged Stallion swoops out from behind the clouds. He bares his teeth in a terrible snarl, then kicks at the band of rebels with his fearsome hooves. There is a sickening crunch as he connects with a rebel's head.

"We've got to fight Malvel!" you say to Tom.

You canter to the tower and push open the doorway at the bottom.

"Wait," says Tom. "Shouldn't we take the rebels up here, too? Skor's too big to fit through the door – they'd be safe."

You want to protect the rebels – but should you and Tom sneak up the tower alone and surprise Malvel?

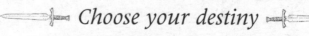 *Choose your destiny*

To go into the tower without the rebels,

*turn to **46**.*

To take the rebels into the tower,

*turn to **35**.*

20

Kaymon's body swells and she splits apart –
becoming three hounds!

One of them springs at Tom, while the
other two circle around you. You manage
to strike the head of one with the hilt of
your sword, knocking her aside, but the
second Kaymon springs at you, her claws
slashing. You leap from her path and she
crashes against the side of the castle.

Panting for breath, you stumble over
something on the ground, in the centre
of the courtyard – a trapdoor.

"Come on!" you yell to Tom, who's
battling the third hound by one of the
pillars. "Let's get out of here!"

You heave the trapdoor open. Tom
crashes his shield into the hound's snout,
and you both dive inside. You charge to the
end of the tunnel and scramble up through
a hatch. With relief, you realise that you've
emerged where you left Storm and
Lightning.

Mounting your horses, you gallop

towards plumes of smoke on the horizon.

"The rebel camp of Kaloom," says Tom. "Maybe they can help with our Quest."

When you reach the camp, you hide the horses and step among the tents. The faces of the rebels are glazed over, like they're in a trance. All the tents are tattered, except for one which you guess must belong to the rebel leader. You go inside.

A hooded figure sits on a velvet chair, his back to you, counting piles of gold.

"What is it?" he grunts.

"We need help," you begin.

The figure drops a handful of coins, and turns round. It's Malvel!

"Well, well," says the Dark Wizard, rubbing his hands delightedly.

Your mind whirls. Could you pretend to support Malvel – or should you use the Horn of Kaloom?

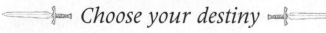 *Choose your destiny*

*To pretend to support Malvel, turn to **24**.*

*To use the horn, turn to **49**.*

21

You and Tom lead the rebel army towards
the Western City, the rebels following
Storm and Lightning on their own horses.
Your path takes you through the Dense
Forest. Moss trails from the gnarled
branches like cobwebs. As you enter a
gloomy clearing, Lightning gives a nervous
whinny.

"Listen," says Tom.

There's a scuffling sound amongst the
trees, and a squeal.

"What's that?" cries one of the rebels,
his eyes wide.

A wild boar suddenly lunges into the
clearing, stabbing with its tusks, its eyes red.
More boars follow, saliva dripping from
their mouths. A rebel screams as
a tusk gouges his leg.

"Go!" you yell.

The rebels follow you in a desperate
charge through the trees. The boars snap
at your heels. You can see bright daylight
ahead and you urge Lightning towards it.

As you thunder out of the forest, the boars snort and slink back into the gloom.

The Western City lies ahead. It's surrounded by jagged walls, its black gates locked. A door is set into the side of the walls, leading to an underground tunnel.

"We can't take the rebels down there – we'd lose people," says Tom. He points to an enormous catapult outside the gates. "Let's use that to get over the walls instead."

⚔ *Choose your destiny* ⚔

To go over the walls with Tom and the rebels,
*turn to **26**.*

*To go into the tunnel alone, turn to **27**.*

You and Tom leave Lightning and Storm
at the side of the moat and wade into the
stagnant water. It's murky and insects buzz
above its surface.

"Urgh," you say, wafting your hand in
front of your nose. "It stinks."

You and Tom wade out until the water
becomes too deep, then start swimming
towards the ruined castle.

Something snares your wrist – a tendril
of pondweed. You shake it away, but the
slimy weed wraps around your arm. You
feel another sliding around your neck,
pulling your face into the water. Tom
struggles beside you, weeds clinging
onto him.

"They're trying to drown us," you gasp.

You tear away the weed around your
arm and pull your sword from its scabbard.
You slash at the weeds and they hiss,
shrivelling away. You and Tom thrash
through the water and drag yourselves
onto the castle flagstones.

"Phew," you gasp. "I thought we'd never—"

But Tom clamps a hand over your mouth. You freeze. Prowling in the courtyard is a Beast. Shaped like a gigantic hound, the muscles of its powerful shoulders ripple and its jaws gape open. Strings of drool hang between its long fangs.

"Kaymon the Gorgon Hound," whispers Tom.

You duck behind a pillar. Kaymon raises her nose, sniffing. Does she sense you're there?

A door is set into the castle wall. Should you run through it and try to find the Dagger – or stay and attack the Beast?

⟵⟶ *Choose your destiny* ⟵⟶

To attack Kaymon, turn to 3.

To run through the doorway, turn to 20.

23

The Dense Forest creaks and groans. You lead the rebels through gloomy clearings, coaxing the horses past thorny bushes and piles of rotten leaves. Your heart flutters anxiously.

"It feels like the trees are watching us," you murmur to Tom.

A crow caws overhead. Out of the corner of your eye you see a flicker of movement. You spin round in Lightning's saddle but there's nothing there – just an old yew tree, its gnarled roots trailing over the earth's surface.

One of the roots lashes out, wrapping around Storm's hind leg. With a terrified neigh he rears up, sending Tom sprawling onto the ground.

You leap down and hack at the root with your sword, freeing Storm. But more roots whip out, snatching Tom and dragging him towards the yew's trunk. The tree starts to tip backwards, the roots rolling Tom underneath it.

"Quick!" you yell to the rebels. "Has anyone got an axe?"

"Here." One of the men darts forward. You snatch the axe from him and heft its blade into one of the roots. It falls away, and you hack through more roots until you and the rebel are able to drag Tom out.

"Thanks," Tom gasps. "Now, let's get out of here."

As you emerge from the forest, the Western City stands before you. The black gates set into its walls are firmly shut. You glance around, searching for a way in. Could you use a tree trunk as a battering ram? Or should you use the gigantic catapult standing near the gate?

====≒ *Choose your destiny* ≒====

To use a battering ram, turn to **19**.

To use a catapult, turn to **26**.

24

You kneel before Malvel. Tom gives you a confused look and you grab his arm, pulling him down beside you.

"Tom and I have been so foolish," you say. "We've only just realised how great you are. We want to fight on your side, Malvel the Magnificent!"

The Dark Wizard strokes his beard. "Malvel the Magnificent, eh? I like it. Very well! You can journey with me to the Western City."

As he strides out of the tent you catch the gleam of something on his belt – the Dagger of Doom, a skull carved into its hilt. You follow him, whispering to Tom. "If we pretend to fight for Malvel, we can get close to the Dagger."

Outside, the rebels stare at you, their eyes glazed and their jaws slack. They bow as Malvel passes, and you realise what's wrong with them – they're under the Dark Wizard's evil thrall. *What if the same thing happens to us?* you think.

Malvel raises his staff, surrounding himself, you and Tom in swirls of blue smoke. With a gasp, you realise that you're floating up above the rebel camp. Lightning and Storm appear beside you, their hooves kicking the air.

"Aren't the rebels coming, Master?" you ask Malvel.

"No," he says. "You two are enough for my purpose."

What could the Dark Wizard mean? Fear trickles down your spine and the blue smoke engulfs you.

When it clears, you're in a tunnel under the city. Torches flicker and stone tombs, like sinister treasure chests, stand against the walls.

"This way," orders Malvel, marching along the tunnel.

Should you hide from him – or follow?

Choose your destiny

To hide from Malvel, turn to **38**.

To follow Malvel, turn to **42**.

25

It's evening. Candles dance among the rebel tents and the air rings with music and laughter.

You and Tom sit with Odora and Kerlo, guests of honour at the celebratory feast. Odora's face is flushed from dancing, and even Kerlo taps his cane in time to the music.

Kerlo gets to his feet. "I must return to my post at the gate, now," he says. His single eye twinkles. "Enjoy the party, young Questers. Find me when you're ready to go home."

Odora glances down at the Dagger of Doom, tucked inside the belt of her dress.

"I still can't believe we've got it back," she says. "How can we ever repay you?"

"You don't have to," Tom says.

You nod in agreement. "While there's blood in our veins, we'll always be ready to fight Malvel!"

The End

26

The catapult is almost as tall as the City walls. Its wooden frame sits on iron wheels, and you, Tom and the rebels push it in front of the gate.

Skor the Winged Stallion circles around the tallest tower of the City. His massive wings beat so powerfully that they blast loose rubble to the ground. He tosses back his head in a mighty roar. "That must be where Malvel is," you say.

"It'll take too long to catapult everyone over the walls," calls a voice from among the crowd of rebels. "Malvel grows stronger with every moment."

The speaker steps forward. It's Kerlo!

He waves his cane at the catapult. "You two should use it, but I'll take the rebels through a tunnel at the back of the City. Leave your horses with me."

"Thanks, Kerlo!" You clap him on the shoulder.

You and Tom clamber into the spoon-like arm of the catapult. Kerlo yanks back the

wooden lever and the arm lurches
forwards, throwing you and Tom into the
air. You soar over the gates, your arms and
legs flailing, and land with a squelch in a
rubbish heap.

"Now we'll stink enough to scare even
Malvel," says Tom with a grin.

You skid down the pile of rubbish, and
race to the tower. The door at the bottom is
open and you run inside, pounding up the
spiral staircase. It's lined with narrow
windows, through which you catch
glimpses of Skor, his teeth bared.

At the top of the staircase is another door. Its surface is covered with metal studs. While Tom yanks at the iron handle, your eye catches something back down the stairs. A tiny bottle stands on the sill of one of the windows, filled with shimmering purple liquid.

"I'm sure that wasn't there a moment ago," you say. "I'm going to get it."

But Tom shakes his head. "Remember what Kerlo said? There isn't time..."

⚔ *Choose your destiny* ⚔

To ignore the bottle, turn to **46**.

To go back and collect the bottle, turn to **56**.

Alone, you hurry through the winding tunnel. At the end is a chamber.

You step inside. In the corner is an enormous heap of bones.

From behind the bone pile steps a terrible Beast. He has a man's shape but his skin is covered in green scales. He picks up one of the bones and bites down on it with his rows of teeth, crunching it to dust.

"Marlik the Drowning Terror is here to help you on the final stage of your Quest," cackles a voice. "Your journey to death!"

You spin round to see Malvel hurl a net at you. It drags you to the ground.

He turns to the Beast. "Finish him off," he says, and hands Marlik a knife – the Dagger of Doom.

The Beast raises the Dagger above your heart...

Your Quest has failed.
And Gorgonia will fall to Malvel...

28

Marlik's arm quivers, the skin becoming transparent as it changes into a swirling column of water. He punches at Tom's throat, the water rolling over your friend's face. Tom gives a terrible, gurgling cry, his eyes rolling back in his head.

He's going to drown, you realise. *I can't save him...*

Blinded with fear, you sprint towards the ruined castle. You stumble in your haste, your feet sliding over the stony ground.

But a webbed hand wraps around your throat. Marlik...

The Beast throws you to the ground. He snarls, his tentacles lashing your face as he raises his watery arm.

There's no escape.

Your Quest has failed.
And Gorgonia will fall to Malvel...

Nervously, you step over the dusty terrain towards Kerlo.

He swivels round on his rock, fixing you with his single eye. "It's about time you arrived," he begins, then jumps to his feet when he sees Odora slumped across Storm's back. He puts his palm to her forehead. "She's very sick," he mutters. "This is Malvel's doing!"

Kerlo explains that Malvel has taken the Dagger of Doom, which a band of rebels forged to protect the realm from his evil. Now the Dark Wizard will easily defeat the rebels, and hold sway over all Gorgonia.

"He has created two new Beasts to stop the rebels getting the Dagger back," Kerlo continues. "One of them must have poisoned your friend."

"Can we help Odora?" Tom asks.

Kerlo shakes his head. "Only magic can save her now. You must take her back to Avantia – to the Good Wizard Aduro."

"Silver and I will go," says Elenna.

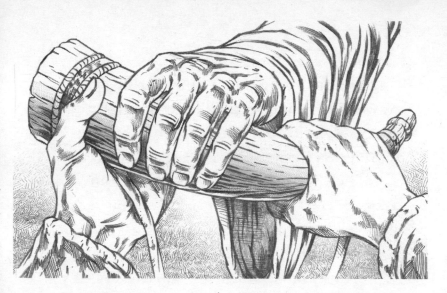

Before you or Tom can protest, she lifts Odora to the ground.

Kerlo says that he'll help them pass back through the gate. He reaches into the folds of his cloak and pulls out a horn carved from bone. "The Horn of Kaloom," he says, passing it to you. "One blast upon it will bring aid. Go, young warriors. May your Quest to stop the Dark Wizard succeed!"

You and Tom wave goodbye to your friends and scramble down the stony slope, leading Storm and Lightning by their reins. At the bottom is a marsh covered in yellow mist. Your feet squelch in the stinking mud.

"Look," says Tom.

He points out two sets of footprints. One shows webbed, human-like feet, and the other, hooves. You wonder if they belong to Malvel's Beasts.

"Which ones should we follow?" Tom asks.

Choose your destiny

*To follow the webbed feet, turn to **47**.*

*To follow the hooves, turn to **15**.*

30

"No," you whisper to Tom. "He isn't
wearing a talisman – we don't know if
we can trust him."

The man turns, and a shiver trickles
down your spine. You would know that
face anywhere. It's Malvel!

The Dark Wizard raises his hands to
the sky, revealing a flash of metal hanging
from his belt. The Dagger!

"I summon you, Skor the Winged
Stallion," Malvel cries.

From your hiding place, you see a flying
horse swoop low over the camp. His
muscular flanks and neck flex as he powers
through the air. With a ferocious roar,

he kicks at the cowering rebels with his huge hooves, and lands beside Malvel. The wizard leaps onto his back.

"To the Western City," orders Malvel, and Skor takes off.

"We've got to go after them," you say.

But should you ask the rebels to come too?

Choose your destiny

To leave the rebels behind, turn to **13**.

To take the rebels with you, turn to **21**.

31

You shake your head. "I'm not fighting you, Malvel," you say.

The Dark Wizard's eyes glitter. "Coward," he spits.

He raises his staff. The tip of it crackles and a blast of energy shoots towards you.

"Run!" yells Tom.

You, Tom and Elenna sprint to the hatch. The blast strikes the floor where you were standing, leaving a smouldering hole.

Tom climbs down the hatch onto the ladder, followed by Elenna.

But as you follow, Malvel snatches up the Dagger of Doom. He hurls it at you and the blade pierces your jerkin, pinning you to the ground.

Panic bubbles inside you as you try to pull away. *I'm trapped*, you realise.

Malvel strides towards you. He kneels beside you, yanking the Dagger free. He raises it to your throat...

Your Quest has failed. And Gorgonia will fall to Malvel...

32

"There's something odd about this boy," you whisper to Tom. "I don't trust him. Let's leave him and find our own way to the castle."

Tom nods. But as you move away, the boy gives a terrible roar. He bounds from the hole, his body twisting and contorting in midair – and turns into a Beast!

He lands in a crouch beside you. His skin is green and scaly, and his hands and feet are webbed. Tentacles swirl about his neck and he gives another roar, revealing row upon row of pointed, deadly teeth.

Malvel's voice echoes inside your head. *Behold my Beast – Marlik the Drowning Terror!*

Marlik springs onto you, knocking you to the ground. His hands wrap around your throat but you hook a foot around his leg, flipping him onto his back. You grab a handful of tentacles, shuddering as they squelch between your fingers, yank his head forwards then slam it into the ground. Marlik gives a furious hiss, and his eyes close.

"He's knocked out – for now," says Tom. "Let's go while we can."

You spot something lying on the ground – a horn. The word "Kaloom" is carved onto it.

You show it to Tom. "Kaloom is where the rebel camp is," he says. "Marlik must have stolen it."

You tuck the horn into your belt, and gallop to the ruined castle. It's surrounded by a stinking green moat. You see a tree growing alongside it, its branches rotten. Perhaps you and Tom could climb up and jump over the moat. Or would it be safer to swim?

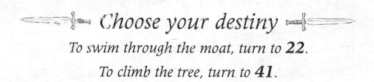

Choose your destiny

*To swim through the moat, turn to **22**.*

*To climb the tree, turn to **41**.*

33

You and Tom step inside the room filled with treasure. It's stuffed with chests brimming over with coins, piles of gems, silver plates and gold statues.

"Malvel must have stolen this from across Gorgonia," you say.

A handful of coins trickles down a glittering gold pile and onto the floor.

You draw your sword. "Who's there?"

But a familiar face emerges from behind the heap of gold. Elenna!

You and Tom rush to hug your friend.

"How did you get here?" Tom asks her. "Through Trillion's portal?"

"No," she replies. "I took Odora to the palace and told Aduro what had happened. He used his magic to send me here. I've searched everywhere in this room for the Dagger, but Malvel must have taken it to the upper levels of the city. Come on!"

You and Tom follow her out of the room and along another tunnel. But there's a jangling noise coming from a nearby chamber.

"It sounds like piles of gems toppling over," says Tom.

"Let's go and grab some," you suggest. "The rebels could use them to buy food."

Elenna shakes her head. "There isn't time. We need to get on with the Quest!"

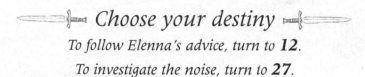 *Choose your destiny*

To follow Elenna's advice, turn to 12.

To investigate the noise, turn to 27.

34

"We should do as the boy asks," Tom whispers.

You nod sadly. The Quest is more important than your bond with Lightning and Storm.

"Goodbye, girl," you murmur, stroking Lightning's head. "Go on, now!"

You give her a gentle push towards the boy. Tom murmurs a farewell in Storm's ear then sends him away as well.

The boy snatches their reins. His eyes blaze and he throws back his head, giving a terrible cry of laughter. The sound makes you feel as though your blood's curdling.

Your horses whinny with fear. The boy roughly shoves them away from him and they gallop, terrified, into the yellow mist.

"That's it," the boy calls after them. "Run away, you stupid nags – and don't come back!"

Then his body swells. His skin turns green and scaly. Tentacles sprout around his neck and pointed teeth jut from his mouth. A clap of thunder splits the sky, and Malvel's voice surrounds you. *Dare you face Marlik the Drowning Terror?*

"He's a Beast," you gasp. You clench your fists, angry with yourself for trusting him.

Marlik lunges towards you and Tom. You leap aside, but the Beast crashes into your friend, pinning him to the ground. Tom's winded, his breath rasping as he struggles to pull away from Marlik's webbed hands.

You draw your sword – then glance towards the ruined castle. It's not too far away. You could run there and get the Dagger while Marlik is distracted...

═══━ *Choose your destiny* ━═══

To run towards the castle, turn to **28**.

To try to save Tom, turn to **55**.

35

You and Tom rush up the spiral stairs,
the rebels behind you. Skor thrusts his
head through the narrow windows,
snatching up men and tossing them
to the ground.

You seize one of the torches hanging
on the wall. When Skor lunges through
another window, you thrust it into his
face. The Beast smashes into the top of
the tower and dissolves into ash.

"You defeated him," cries Tom, clapping
you on the shoulder.

You sprint to the top of the stairs. Malvel
lies under the rubble from the top of the
tower, his staff out of his reach.

The rebels crowd around him. "Let's
finish him off," says one.

But you shake your head. "Enough blood
has been spilt. Malvel, we'll free you –
but only if you hand over the Dagger."

Malvel scowls, but he pulls out the
Dagger and gives it to you. At your
command, the rebels lift the rubble away

and he disappears in a flash of blue flame.

The Quest is over!

You and Tom make your way out of the tower. The air shimmers and the portal of Trillion's jaws appears.

Tom grins. "It's time to go home."

But the air shimmers again and another portal appears. This one looks like a snake's jaws. Which should you choose?

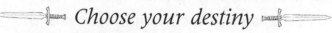 *Choose your destiny*

*To go through Trillion's jaws, turn to **10**.*

*To go through the snake's jaws, turn to **44**.*

36

Leaving Storm and Lightning on the banks of the moat, you and Tom step into the small rowing boat bobbing in the stagnant green water. Two paddles lie inside; you each take one and push off from the shore. You see dark shadows under the surface of the water – evil fish with sharp teeth poking from their mouths.

"Look," says Tom, pointing to the courtyard in the castle.

You stop rowing. An enormous dog-like Beast is prowling over the flagstones. Her muscular body ripples and drool pours from her enormous jaws. Her hackles are raised and her eyes flash with fury.

"I've fought her before," says Tom. "It's Kaymon the Gorgon Hound."

"Let's steer round to the back of the castle," you say. "Maybe she won't see us."

But the wooden planks at the bottom of the boat snap. Your foot plunges into the foul water.

"The wood's rotten!" you cry.

As the boat disintegrates, you see the deadly looking fish start to circle. You have no choice but to swim to shore – whether Kaymon sees you or not.

You both plunge into the water. A fish bites onto your arm, and when you swat it away a thread of blood floats from your punctured skin. As you near the castle, Kaymon spots you. Her tail swishes and she lets out a growl that echoes around you like an earthquake.

Dripping wet and covered in slime, you heave yourself into the castle courtyard. To the side is an open door, set into the crumbling walls. Should you run through it – or stay and face the Beast?

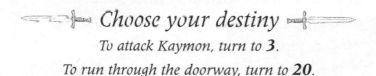 *Choose your destiny*
To attack Kaymon, turn to 3.
To run through the doorway, turn to 20.

37

"You're right," you say to Tom. "We might just summon more enemies if we use the horn."

You glance down to slide the horn back into your belt. But Marlik sees that you're distracted and leaps on you. The Beast's weight crushes you into the muddy swamp.

"No!" yells Tom.

Marlik's webbed hands grip your shoulders. Your arms and legs flounder, but you can't break free. The Beast becomes transparent, the surface of his body rippling. He's turned into water!

With a roar like waves crashing against rock, the Beast thrusts one of his arms down your throat. You feel the gushing water flood your nose, your lungs...

A mocking voice fills your head. Malvel!

Fool, sneers the Dark Wizard. *Prepare yourself for death*.

Your Quest has failed. And Gorgonia will fall to Malvel...

38

"Where can we hide?" Tom asks.

Your gaze falls on one of the stone tombs that line the tunnel. Tom shudders.

"We don't have any other choice," you say.

You send the horses back along the tunnel, trusting them to find their way out. Then you and Tom approach the tomb. It's almost as high as your shoulders and covered in a flat stone lid.

"Here goes," you mutter. You grip the edge of the lid and slide it open. Dust billows out and inside is a heap of bones.

Gritting your teeth, you climb in and lie down. Tom follows and you pull the lid back.

In the darkness, you hear footsteps approach.

"Malvel," Tom whispers.

They seem to stop next to the tomb. You hold your breath.

With a groan, the lid slides backwards. You leap up, your sword raised, but there's an arrow pressed to your throat.

"Elenna!" Tom cries.

She lowers her bow, grinning with relief. "I'm so glad I've found you. Come on – the Dagger's this way!"

She dashes down the tunnel. Tom grabs your arm before you can follow.

"How do we know she's really Elenna?" he whispers. "What if she's a vision conjured by Malvel?"

⊰⊱ *Choose your destiny* ⊰⊱

To follow Elenna, turn to 12.

To go in the opposite direction, turn to 27.

39

"Alright, Malvel," you say. "I accept."

Tom shakes his head. "What if it's a trap?"

But you shrug off Tom's concerns and raise your sword.

Malvel grabs his staff. "I'm going to enjoy this."

His staff crackles with blue light and a bolt of energy shoots straight at you. You jump onto the table and it strikes the cauldron, making it explode into sizzling flames.

The Dark Wizard laughs. "That was just a warm up."

He pulls the Dagger from the table and strikes it against your sword. Malvel twists his arm, forcing you to drop your blade. He backs you up against the wall. "Prepare to die," the Dark Wizard mocks. A fleck of his saliva hits your cheek.

Malvel draws the Dagger back. But as he slams it towards your chest, you step aside.

The blade thuds into the wall. Malvel

snarls furiously and Tom grabs your sword
and throws it to you. You strike the wizard
on the side of his head with the flat of the
blade. His eyes roll back and he slumps to
the floor.

Panting for breath, you grab the Dagger.
Tom and Elenna grin.

"You did it!" Tom cries.

The three of you sprint from the
banqueting room and out into the streets.
The air shimmers and the portal made from
Trillion's jaws appears. Aduro steps through
it – then Odora.

She smiles as you pass her the Dagger. "I'll deliver it to the rebels," she says. "Thanks to you, Gorgonia is safe from Malvel."

Aduro's eyes twinkle. "It's time to go home."

With a puff of smoke, the Good Wizard makes Storm and Lightning appear. Waving farewell to Odora, you all step through the portal.

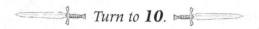 *Turn to* **10**.

40

You scramble up the desolate hillside, away from Kerlo.

"I don't think he can see us up here," you say, stopping by a pile of boulders.

Odora groans and sits up in Storm's saddle.

"You're awake!" cries Elenna, helping her to the ground. Silver gives a delighted bark.

Odora rubs her eyes as if amazed at the sight of you and your companions. "I'm so glad you've come to help us," she says. "Gorgonia is in great danger."

She explains that Malvel has stolen the Dagger of Doom from the rebels.

"It's made from a magical metal that protects us from his evil," Odura says. "We've got to get it back – or Malvel will soon take over Gorgonia."

Tom frowns. "We need to tell King Hugo and Wizard Aduro what Malvel's up to. Avantia could be in danger, too."

"I'll go back," Elenna says. "With Odora –

and Silver, of course."

"Are you sure?" you ask.

Elenna nods and claps you on the shoulder. "Positive! I can't think of a better Quest companion for Tom than you."

You wave goodbye as Elenna, Odora and Silver hurry back to the gate. Then you and Tom set off down the dusty slope.

Ahead of you stands a boy. He's short and skinny, but leaps easily over the rocks. "This way!" he calls. "I'll lead you into Gorgonia."

You follow him along a path that cuts away from the hillside. Tom gives a shout of excitement.

"You're a Gorgonian rebel!" He points to

the silver talisman hanging round the boy's neck. "Do you know Odora?"

The boy looks blank for a moment, then says, "Of course. Why wouldn't I?"

The air thickens and turns into a sickly yellow mist. Just visible on the horizon is a ruined castle.

"Malvel's holding the Dagger there," the boy says. "The way to the castle is deadly. I'll show you – if you give up your horses to the rebel cause."

You glance at Tom. This is your chance to complete the Quest. But can you say goodbye to Lightning and Storm?

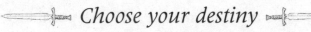 *Choose your destiny*

To refuse to hand over the horses, turn to **6**.

To hand the horses over, turn to **34**.

41

Storm and Lightning watch as you and
Tom clamber up the tree that stands
alongside the moat, their ears flicking
nervously. The tree's branches are black
and bare of leaves, while the bark is
covered in a sheen of grease.

One of the branches extends over the
moat. You clamber onto it.

"If we climb to the end we can leap
through there," you call to Tom, pointing
at a window placed halfway up one of the
turrets.

You crawl along the branch. But your
grip slips on the greasy bark and you fall,
clinging desperately with one hand, your
legs dangling beneath you.

"Hold on," shouts Tom. He scrambles
over, seizing your other hand and pulling
you up.

When you reach the end of the branch,
you carefully stand upright and jump,
soaring through the window and rolling
to your feet. Tom follows. You're in a dark

chamber with two lights glowing in the shadows.

The lights move and you follow them out of the chamber, down a spiral staircase, feeling your way through the darkness. Then they disappear and you can see daylight ahead. You emerge through a door and out into the castle courtyard – and freeze with horror.

The lights are the glowing eyes of a ferocious, dog-like Beast. Its hackles are raised, its teeth bared. It paws the ground, ready to spring at you.

"Kaymon the Gorgon Hound," breathes Tom, his face white.

Should you stay and attack her? Or run back into the turret?

Choose your destiny

To attack Kaymon, turn to **3**.
To run back into the turret, turn to **20**.

42

You gently push Lightning and Storm back down the tunnel.

"Go and wait for us outside," you murmur. You and Tom might be following Malvel, but it's too dangerous for your horses.

The Dark Wizard leads you down a long corridor lined with suits of armour. His cloak streams out behind him, its reflection dancing on the gleaming metal breastplates and helmets.

Something else moves among the suits of armour, too – a person, darting through the shadows...

You nudge Tom. "We're being watched," you whisper. "It must be one of Malvel's spies."

But the figure waves to you. "Psst! It's me."

Elenna!

Malvel swings around a corner and you follow, Elenna keeping close to the wall.

"How did you get here?" you whisper.

"Aduro's magic," she replies.

You take Tom's elbow, drawing him away from her. "Don't you think this is a bit strange?" you whisper. "Why would Elenna just appear like this?"

Tom's eyes widen as he stares at his old friend. "Do you think she's under Malvel's spell?"

Elenna beckons you towards her again. "Malvel's leading you into a trap. Come this way!" She darts into a side-chamber.

You and Tom glance at each other. Should you do as she says?

Choose your destiny

To follow Elenna, turn to **12**.

To keep following Malvel, turn to **27**.

43

"We're looking for the Dagger of Doom,"
you tell the soothsayer. "Can you help us
find it?"

Her wrinkled face darkens with anger.
"If you don't do as I say, then I can't
help you."

She hobbles away among the castle
ruins.

Tom sighs. "We should have listened
to her."

But you've spotted a glassy ball on the
ground. "Her seeing stone! She must have
dropped it."

An image forms inside the glass, showing
rows of tents.

"The rebel camp of Kaloom," Tom says.
"The Dagger could be there."

Beside the seeing stone is an iron ring,
set into one of the flagstones. You pull it,
and the flagstone lifts. It's a trapdoor! You
climb down into a narrow tunnel,
emerging on the other side of the moat,
where Storm and Lightning are waiting.

You gallop to the rebel camp. From behind a clump of trees, you and Tom watch the rebels milling around the tents. Your fingers close over the Horn of Kaloom hanging at your belt.

"Maybe we should use the horn," you suggest. "The rebels might help our Quest."

Tom looks thoughtful. "We can't be sure Malvel's evil hasn't got here first. We should watch the camp, just in case."

⚔ Choose your destiny ⚔

To use the horn, turn to 5.

To spy on the rebel camp, turn to 17.

44

You, Tom, Storm and Lightning step through the portal. Your foot snares on one of the snake fangs, but you smile. *In a few moments, we'll be back home...*

You feel the same surge of energy pass through you as when you entered Gorgonia. You close your eyes against the blinding white light, but when you open them again, you and your companions are surrounded by flames. The air is thick with smoke.

"This isn't Avantia!" you cry. "What's happened?"

Malvel's mocking laughter echoes around you, and despite the heat from the flames, a chill passes down your spine.

"Fools!" sneers the Dark Wizard. "You may have the Dagger, but did you really think you could defeat me?"

"No!" you cry – but there's no escape. The snake's jaws were Malvel's final trick.

The smoke coils down your throat, making your eyes stream and your chest tightens. You slump to the ground. Flames lick around you, and you smell the acrid stench of your own burning flesh.

Your Quest has failed. And Gorgonia will fall to Malvel...

45

You leap from Lightning's saddle and lead her onto the rickety drawbridge. Tom does the same with Storm, but the wooden planks groan.

"It's not strong enough," says Tom.

You leave the horses on the bank and walk across instead. Between the planks you see the green water swirl. Evil-looking fish swim through it, fangs jutting from their mouths.

Creak! The plank you're standing on splits and your leg shoots through the gap, trailing into the water. The fish dart towards you, their jaws snapping.

Tom grabs your arm and heaves you back onto the drawbridge. You sprint to the castle, the rest of the bridge collapsing behind you. Throwing yourself through a stone archway, you gasp for breath.

"Come on," pants Tom.

You draw your swords and step into a courtyard. It's edged by half-fallen pillars and is overlooked by crumbling turrets.

You both start as a stone rolls out from behind a pillar, rattling across the flagstones.

"Who's there?" you call.

An old woman steps out. Her face is creased with wrinkles and she wears a black cape, a crystal clutched in her hand.

"That's a seeing stone," Tom whispers. "She must be a soothsayer – one who sees the future."

You both step towards the woman. "Can you help us? We're—"

"Silence!" she interrupts. She gestures with a gnarled finger for you to follow. "I have something to show you," she says.

You move after her, but Tom catches your arm.

"Shouldn't we ask her about the Dagger?" he whispers.

⇒ *Choose your destiny* ⇐

To follow the soothsayer, turn to **9**.

To ask the soothsayer about the Dagger,

turn to **43**.

46

"Push!" you yell.

You and Tom lean against the door at the top of the tower, forcing it open. It leads onto the roof. At the centre stands Malvel, the Dagger of Doom in his hand.

"Foolish Questers," he sneers, "I've won!"

You glance at Tom. "Charge!" you yell.

You both rush at the Dark Wizard. But he uses the Dagger like a sword, forcing you to the edge of the roof. You hear the beating of wings.

You spin round. Skor is diving down at you, his jaws wide open.

"No!" you yell.

Skor's teeth close around your arm. He lifts you from the tower, soaring over the Western City, then lets go. As you plummet towards the ground, the last sound you hear is the Dark Wizard's mocking laughter.

Your Quest has failed. And Gorgonia will fall to Malvel...

47

You and Tom splash through the foul swamp, leading Lightning and Storm by their bridles. The mud clings to your feet and yellow mist swirls around you.

Lightning gives an anxious neigh.

"I know, girl," you say, stroking her velvety muzzle. "There's something strange about this place."

Ahead of you, Tom coaxes Storm along. But his horse slithers into a deeper patch of mud, sinking up to his knees.

"No!" Tom shouts. Storm whinnies with distress.

A figure appears through the yellow mist. It's a man dressed in a leather jerkin, a coil of rope hanging at his waist.

You draw your sword. "Who are you?"

The man raises his hands. "I'm unarmed, strangers." He points to Storm. "Looks like you need my help."

The man kneels beside Storm, murmuring to the struggling horse. He takes the rope from his waist – and you

see that his hands are green, with webbed
skin stretched between the fingers.

You hurl yourself at him, knocking him
away from Storm.

The man cackles. "Almost fooled, weren't
you? Marlik the Drowning Terror is here..."

His body contorts and turns green.
Tentacles grow from his neck. He roars,
the sound echoing through you. Inside his
open jaws you see hundreds of fangs. *He's
a Beast...*

Marlik moves towards Storm, drool
trickling down his chin. You need help!
You reach for the horn at your belt.

But Tom stays your hand. "It might just
summon more Beasts!"

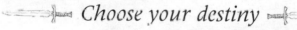 *Choose your destiny*

To sound a blast on the horn, turn to **50**.
To decide not to use the horn, turn to **37**.

48

You leap up, grabbing the branch. You wince as the thorns cut into your fingers, but tighten your grip, raising your legs as Klaxa charges underneath you. Her deadly horn just misses your feet.

Phew, you think, and try to drop to the ground. But the thorns are gripping your hands. Horrified, you see more thorns sprout from the branch and wrap around your wrists. It's as if the land itself is fighting you...

"Look out!" yells Tom.

You twist round to see Klaxa lower her head and charge at you again. You raise your feet as she passes under, then drive your heels onto the back of her neck.

Klaxa gives a furious roar.

Tom darts forwards, grabbing your sword. He leaps up, striking the thorny branch with both blades. It withers, and you fall free.

Before Klaxa can recover, you mount your horses and gallop away through the mist. In the distance you see a ruined castle.

"That looks like the kind of place where Malvel would hide the Dagger," you say.

You gallop towards it. The castle is circled by a putrid moat. A ladder made from bone leads from the bank to one of the turrets, and in the water bobs a boat. How should you get into the castle?

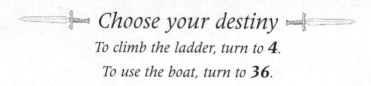 *Choose your destiny*

To climb the ladder, turn to **4**.

To use the boat, turn to **36**.

49

"Guards! Seize them!" Malvel yells. His lips curl into a sneer. "I'll have fun dealing with you two later."

Four guards rush into the tent, their eyes glazed over. Two of them grab Tom's arms, forcing them behind his back, but before they can seize you, you pull the horn from your belt and sound a ringing blast.

Malvel claps his hands over his ears, wincing. The guards' eyes brighten. They release Tom, their jaws dropping with horror as they stare at Malvel.

"You're free from his spell, now," you tell them.

Malvel's face is purple with fury. Snatching up his staff, he fires a bolt of magic at one of the guards. You leap in front of him, blocking it with your shield. There are shouts outside and Malvel rushes from the tent. You, Tom and the guards follow.

The rebels' eyes are clear and you and Tom exchange a grin.

"It's as if they've been brought back to life," you say.

One of the rebels points to Malvel. "There he is! He's using his magic to take Gorgonia!"

The Dark Wizard fires a dazzling blast. "Silence," he roars, "before I kill you all."

He pulls something out from his belt and waves it to you and Tom – a blade with a skull carved into the hilt. The Dagger of Doom!

"Looking for this?" he asks mockingly, then disappears in a puff of black smoke.

"He'll have gone to the Western City," says one of the guards. "That's where his lair is."

You and Tom must follow – but should you take the rebels with you? They could help your Quest, but you might be putting them in terrible danger...

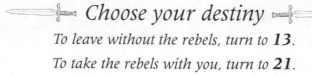

Choose your destiny

*To leave without the rebels, turn to **13**.*

*To take the rebels with you, turn to **21**.*

50

You raise the horn to your lips and sound
a mighty blast. It echoes across the swamp.

Marlik's webbed hands wrap around
Storm's neck and dunk his head under the
mud. Storm's legs thrash. You and Tom
each seize Marlik, but you can't pull
him away.

Crack! A long, sharp object strikes
Marlik's shoulder. With a howl, he releases
Storm, and you recognise the weapon as
Kerlo's cane.

As you and Tom pull Storm upright, the
Gatekeeper emerges through the mist.

"Get back, foul Beast!" Kerlo yells.

He grabs his cane and whips Marlik's
scaly back. The Beast springs away and
lunges at you, knocking you to the
ground. He snarls, revealing hundreds
of jagged teeth.

As Marlik brings his jaws down to your
neck, you scoop up a slimy handful of mud
and stuff it into his mouth. The Beast
chokes, rolling away.

"Go now," Kerlo insists, pulling you to your feet. "Malvel is at the ruined castle."

"What about the Beast?" you ask, panting for breath.

"Leave him to me," Kerlo says. "Go!"

When you reach the castle, you see that it's circled by a stagnant moat. A rickety drawbridge crosses it, and a line of rocks stick up through the water. Which way into the castle should you choose?

Choose your destiny

*To go over the drawbridge, turn to **45**.*

*To go over the rocks, turn to **52**.*

51

"Help!" Tom yells from the battlements. One of the Kaymons has his arm in her jaws, while the other crouches, ready to pounce.

You ignore his cries. Grabbing the iron ring, you heave open the trapdoor and step inside. A flight of steps is cut into the earth and you hurry down them into a tunnel. As you walk away from the castle, the light cast by the trapdoor entrance fades. It becomes utterly dark.

A bloodcurdling roar echoes down the tunnel, followed by the crash of rock. The Kaymon you were fighting must have freed herself!

You sprint down the tunnel, fear prickling over your skin. There's a dot of light ahead. *If I can just reach it...*

But heavy footsteps thud into the tunnel. You look back and see the glowing eyes of the Beast, gleaming through the darkness. You run, your lungs burning and your legs pounding, but Kaymon easily catches up.

Her breath rasps and with a swipe of one of her enormous paws she knocks you to the ground.

Her teeth sink into your throat.

Your Quest has failed. And Gorgonia will fall to Malvel...

52

You leave Storm and Lightning by the bank
and step onto the first rock that juts from
the water, holding your arms out for
balance.

"This is easy!" you call over your
shoulder to Tom.

You spring from rock to rock. The one
in the middle of the moat is far larger than
the others. You leap onto it – and it starts
to shudder...

The rock rises up from the water, and
with a jolt of fear, you realise you're
crouching on the back of a Beast! Its flanks
are covered with thick bony hide, and
a huge horn juts from its forehead.

You jump as you hear Malvel's voice,
winding about you like a poisonous gas.
Klaxa the Armoured Enemy is here...

The huge muscles of Klaxa's neck and
shoulders ripple as she gives an ear-
splitting roar. Then she rears up and you
topple into the moat. Klaxa swipes her
deadly horn at Tom, sending him splashing

beneath the surface.

We can't fight in the water, you think
desperately.

The Beast looks around, confused.
She's searching for Tom!

He re-emerges, spluttering.

"Swim underwater," you yell to him.
"Then the Beast can't see us."

You both take a deep breath and dive
under. Opening your eyes, you peer
through the green film. Klaxa's huge legs

thrash about. You spot the stone buttresses of the castle and swim towards them, scrambling ashore. Klaxa is still twisting around, searching the moat for you.

"Welcome," says a creaking voice.

An old woman stands in the castle courtyard, a crystal in her hand.

"That's a seeing stone," whispers Tom. "She must be a soothsayer."

She curls a finger, gesturing towards a turret. Inside is a spiral staircase.

⫸ *Choose your destiny* ⫷

To follow the soothsayer upstairs, turn to **9**.
To refuse to follow the soothsayer, turn to **16**.

53

You flick up the fabric wall of the tent
with your elbow, and you and Tom crawl
underneath. You're in luck – your
confiscated swords and shields are lying
outside the tent. You use the edge of your
sword to cut through your bonds, while
Tom does the same.

As you leap to your feet, you notice that
the rebels' glassy eyes are looking towards
the sky. A shadow appears across the
clouds. It's a flying horse, beating the air
with powerful wings, its teeth snapping.
Its massive hooves are like clubs.

"Skor the Winged Stallion," Tom says.
"I've had to fight him before."

Skor swoops through the camp, kicking
rebels aside with his hooves. He bears
down on an old man, backing him up
against one of the tents.

"Leave him alone!" you cry. You and
Tom surge forwards, parrying Skor's
kicking hooves with your shields. The
Beast lifts into the air.

The old man's eyes fix on the horn hanging from your belt – and they brighten and clear. "The Horn of Kaloom," he mutters. "I see it now – Malvel must have put us under his spell..."

Skor lands and Malvel strides out from between the tents. You and Tom duck behind a pile of cooking pots. In the Dark Wizard's hand is a blade, a skull carved into its hilt. The Dagger of Doom! Malvel leaps onto Skor's back, ordering him to go to the Western City.

"We've got to follow and get the Dagger back," Tom says.

You glance down at the horn, thinking about its effect on the old man. Does it have the power to release the rebels from Malvel's thrall? Should you risk trying?

⟫⟩ *Choose your destiny* ⟨⟪

To use the horn to try to free the rebels,

turn to **2**.

To persuade the rebels to follow you without

using the horn, turn to **23**.

54

"I'm coming, Tom!" You sprint up a staircase to the jagged battlements. One of the Kaymons has its jaws wrapped around his arm, while another is crouched, ready to spring.

With a cry, you charge at the crouching Kaymon, slashing her furry hide with your sword. She leaps towards you, roaring, and you drop to the ground. She sails right over you, rolling down the staircase and landing in a crumpled heap in the courtyard.

Tom gives a cry of pain as the third Beast tightens its grip. You leap onto the battlement wall. "Over here!" you yell.

The Beast lunges up at you. You jump down from the battlements and she tumbles over them. Her claws scrabble at the edge of the wall, but she falls into the moat with a splash.

"Are you alright?" you ask Tom.

He nods, rubbing his arm. "Thanks. Let's go!"

You run down to the courtyard and show Tom the trapdoor in the centre. You climb down, into a tunnel. Insects cling to the ceiling, their tails giving off a pale green light.

"Glow worms," you say. "They look magical."

But one falls from the ceiling, bursting into flame. More glow-worms plop down, exploding into burning flares.

"Run!" you cry, dodging the ever-growing patches of fire.

There's a passageway at the side of the

tunnel and you dive into it. At the end is
a door. You go through, and emerge into
a network of tunnels.

"We're under the Western City," you say.

"Far from Storm and Lightning," Tom
adds. "I hope we'll be able to go back for
them."

Before you are two gleaming rooms.
One is filled with armour, the other with
treasure. Which way should you go?

Choose your destiny

To go into the room filled with armour,

turn to 7.

To go into the room filled with treasure,

turn to 33.

55

You charge at Marlik and he tosses Tom
aside and punches you in the stomach.
Dropping your sword and shield, you
stagger back.

As the Beast advances on you, you
stumble over something in the mud. It's
a horn carved from bone. Snatching it up,
you strike Marlik across his scaly face.
He slumps into the mud, growling.

You notice a word carved on the side
of the horn. "Kaloom," you read.

"That's where the rebel camp is," says
Tom, standing up stiffly and wiping the
mud from his clothes. "Maybe Marlik
stole it."

"We should go before he comes round,"
you say. You slide the horn into your belt
and whistle for Storm and Lightning. They
appear out of the mist and you gallop
towards a distant ruined castle.

"Let's search for the Dagger," suggests
Tom.

The castle is surrounded by a moat.

Should you swim through the putrid water
or climb the tree that hangs over it and
jump to the other side?

⟢ *Choose your destiny* ⟣

To swim the moat, turn to **22**.

To climb the tree, turn to **41**.

Putting the bottle in your pocket, you help Tom force the door open.

It leads to the roof of the tower. Skor circles overhead. In the centre is Malvel, standing over a bubbling cauldron. The Dagger of Doom glitters in his belt.

"Too late!" the Dark Wizard crows. "My potion is almost ready. I just need to add the dissolving liquid."

Tom gasps. "You're going to destroy the Dagger. Then the rebels will never be safe from you!"

"That's right." Malvel feels inside his cloak, frowning.

Your heart thumping with excitement, you take the bottle from your pocket. "Lost something?" you ask, waving it at Malvel.

Panic flickers in the Dark Wizard's eyes. "Attack!" he yells to Skor.

You flick the cork stopper from the bottle. As the Beast dives at you, you shake some of the dissolving liquid over him. Skor gives a shriek of pain and melts before your eyes until he has completely disappeared.

You walk towards Malvel. "I'll destroy you too if you don't hand over the Dagger."

Malvel passes it to you. But then he grabs his staff. "Die, fools!" he yells.

Suddenly, a cane hurtles through the air, knocking the staff to the ground.

"Kerlo!" you cry. The Gatekeeper is in the doorway, the rebels behind him.

"Get out of my way," hisses Malvel, pushing through the crowd.

The air quivers and the portal made from Trillion's jaws appears. Aduro steps through it. Odora is behind him, fully healed. You pass her the Dagger.

"Your Quest is over," the Good Wizard says. "It's time to go home."

Odora smiles. "Or you could celebrate here with us."

Choose your destiny

To go home, turn to **10**.

To stay in Gorgonia to celebrate, turn to **25**.

Join the Quest,
Join the Tribe

www.beastquest.co.uk

Have you checked out the all-new Beast Quest website?
It's the place to go for games, downloads, activities,
sneak previews and lots of fun!

You can read all about your favourite beasts, download
free screensavers and desktop wallpapers for your
computer, and even challenge your friends
to a Beast Tournament.

Sign up to the newsletter at www.beastquest.co.uk
to receive exclusive extra content and the opportunity
to enter special members-only competitions. We'll send
you up-to-date info on all the Beast Quest books,
including the next exciting series which features
six brand new Beasts!

All books priced at £4.99,
special bumper editions
priced at £5.99.

Orchard Books are available from all good bookshops, or can
be ordered from our website: www.orchardbooks.co.uk,
or telephone 01235 827702, or fax 01235 8227703.

Series 8: THE PIRATE KING
COLLECT THEM ALL!

BALISK
THE WATER SNAKE

978 1 40831 310 7

KORON
JAWS OF DEATH

978 1 40831 311 4

HELTON
THE BODY SNATCHER

978 1 40831 312 1

TORNO
THE HURRICANE DRAGON

978 1 40831 313 8

KRONUS
THE CLAWED MENACE

978 1 40831 314 5

BLOODBOAR
THE BURIED DOOM

978 1 40831 315 2

Sanpao the Pirate King wants to steal the magical
Tree of Being. Can Tom scupper his plans?

Series 9: THE WARLOCK'S STAFF

URSUS
THE CLAWED BEAR
978 1 40831 316 9

MINOS
THE DEMON BULL
978 1 40831 317 6

KORAKA
THE WINGED ASSASSIN
978 1 40831 318 3

SILVER
THE WILD TERROR
978 1 40831 319 0

SPIKEFIN
THE WATER KING
978 1 40831 320 6

TORPIX
THE TWISTING SERPENT
978 1 40831 321 3

SPECIAL BUMPER EDITION!

Watch out for Raksha the Mirror Demon...

BEAST QUEST
SPECIALS

978 1 84616 951 9

978 1 84616 994 6

978 1 40830 382 5

978 1 40830 436 5

978 1 40830 735 9

978 1 40830 736 6

978 1 40831 027 4

Join Tom and his brave companions for these
Beast Quest special bumper editions, with
two stories in one!